Rebecca Jessen was born in Orange and grew up in Western Sydney. In 2011 she graduated from the Queensland University of Technology with a Bachelor of Fine Arts in Creative Writing. In 2012 Rebecca won the State Library of Queensland Young Writers Award for her short story *Gap*. In 2013 she won the Queensland Literary Award for Best Emerging Author for the novelisation of *Gap*.

PREVIOUS WINNERS OF THE QUEENSLAND LITERARY AWARD FOR BEST EMERGING AUTHOR

REBECCA**GAP**JESSEN

First published 2014 by University of Queensland Press
PO Box 6042, St Lucia, Queensland 4067 Australia

www.uqp.com.au
uqp@uqp.uq.edu.au

Cover design by Sandy Cull, gogoGingko
Typeset in 11/14pt Bembo by Post Pre-press Group, Brisbane
Printed in Australia by McPherson's Printing Group

 This project has been assisted by the Australian
Government through the Australia Council for
the Arts, its arts funding and advisory body.

Cataloguing-in-Publication entry is available
from the National Library of Australia
http://catalogue.nla.gov.au

ISBN
978 0 7022 53201 (pbk)
978 0 7022 52815 (pdf)
978 0 7022 52822 (epub)
978 0 7022 52839 (Kindle)

University of Queensland Press uses papers that are
natural, renewable and recyclable products made from
wood grown in sustainable forests. The logging and
manufacturing processes conform to the environmental
regulations of the country of origin.

FOR MY SISTER, OLIVIA

PART ONE
DOWN AGAIN

Looking on the streets
for the hangers-on

never know
who's lurking round these parts

seen me leave his house
round the back

pale and sweaty
what have I done?

Walk the twenty minutes home
from his to mine

these paths I remember
all too well

happy for the busted streetlights
tonight

done with the letters
to council

keep the lights out.

Didn't mean to do it

now I've wasted
years of getting back
on track
now I'll spend years
getting over it

tell myself
it was the only way

he made threats

on my life
on Indie

my kid sister
caught up in
my mess again

not too different
to Mum after all.

Back to my territory
the Gabba lights
illuminating the sky

good old Park Rd railway
no one round these parts

not at night
no one so stupid

pull myself over the rusted wire
they forgot about this place

grass grows too high
enveloping the weeds

rotted sleepers
that would split
if you kicked hard enough.

Haven't seen rain in months

grass looks like wheat
scratching at my legs
as I tramp through

gotta get out of here
before the 11 o'clock train

take it out
of my backpack

throw it into the overgrown scrub

wouldn't look here
won't come looking for me.

Fields of wheat
seen on family car trips
we hadn't taken
since

I was too young
to know what I'd turn into

since
Indie was still
falling at my feet.

Best bit about Park Rd
walking through the side streets
where no one's looking
out for you

on any other night
it would have me
looking over my shoulder
but tonight

I'm slumped into myself
like I've just been
kicked in the stomach.

Stumbled home from this train station
too many times

with a girl
but mostly

alone
wasted
forgetting.

I haven't ever done
anything like this

will that hold up
to the suits?

and the yes please
no sir
pass the water thanks?

got a history
but who doesn't?

self-defence

they'll find holes in my story
but I'll cry poor

didn't mean to see the bastard
dead

just a warning
one he was never gonna
forget.

Been in trouble before
petty stuff

stolen
from petty people

got mixed up
with the kind of crowd
I'd take home to my mother

something pulled me out of it
slapped me hard

Indie

working two jobs now
stumbling among
dead weeds

took a long time
finding my way back
from what I used to be.

The nights aren't
normally

cold
like this

wrap my arms
round my trembling body

might not be the cold
after all.

Guess us girls
got Mum's luck

shit
that is

cops on the doorstep
our *Saturday Disney*

tell myself
Mum tried hard

I tell Indie anyway
kid's too young
to know otherwise.

Usually find me
flailing
in my own shadow

tonight's no different

got me caught up
two doors down

jumping at the sight
of the dark behind me.

Lights still on
what's my excuse
worked back

someone has to pay the bills
don't say that though
Indie's heard it enough

'Hey, Ana'
she's watching *Rage* again
'Where you been?'

'Work, keep it down
don't stay up late'
this kid's too smart

head to the bedroom
dump the backpack
lock myself in

how am I gonna get out
this mess.

Indie rages
'til one

start to sweat again
thinking

she'll come in
for her clothes
or to sleep

keep thinking

pull out the sofa Indie
don't check on me
don't get changed
just go to sleep

don't want you to see me

lying in the dark
wet-eyed
heart-wrenched.

Listen to her routine
peels herself off the
cheap vinyl couch

turns off the TV
listen to the static crackle

flicks the switch
remembers what I told her
saving power is
saving money

another switch
awful sound of
the sofa bed

limbs stretched.

3 a.m. and I'm tired
already
of the feeling
that these walls
just got a whole lot smaller

gonna wrap
around us

any day
any time

take Indie away
back to the shit
back to Mum

couldn't do it to her
done it to myself.

Run my fingers
down my legs

still brown from last summer
still tired
from all the running

trace the scratches
skin already raised and red

have to stop stumbling.

'Morning' Indie says
head down
in a bowl of fruit loops

I nod
slump in the creaky chair
five bucks at the local
Lifeline

told Indie I'd make her feel
at home

she pushes the cereal box
can't stomach it

concentrate instead
on the word maze
do they make these things childproof?

'What are you doing today?' Indie says
I'm still looking for that damn word

she kicks me under the table
'Nothing, work
you need to study
got your Year 10 exams coming up
and keep off this stuff
how you gonna function
with all that sugar?'

I snatch up the box
'Grouch' Indie says
as I walk
into the bedroom.

Hole in my favourite shirt
Indie got it for my
twenty-third birthday

what am I gonna tell her
sorry kid

ripped it on
rusted wire fence

trying to hide
the evidence.

Mum did her best
that's what I say

loser dad
dropped out of our lives

too young to notice
I didn't tell her
that I blame
Mum

her and her dropkick
boyfriends
who let me
snatch beers
sniff drugs

get addicted
then
kicked me out of the house

sixteen with no hope
couldn't stay in school

kid sister Indie
stuck with them

didn't ever think
life could shift

didn't ever think
I'd lift the stains
from the walls

don't know how Indie kept her mind
in a place
like that.

Mum always said
get a job Ana
you raise yourselves

see how easy it is

what you gonna do
with an education?

us Robertson kids never read books
think you're special?
that you got something to give
more than we do?

dropkick boyfriend
laughed
snorted

made a groove in the couch
with his ignorance

decided to let Mum
sink in too

but not Indie
kid's too smart for our shit
she's still got hope.

Get outta here
Mum's screaming like a madwoman

sure the neighbours knew
think they locked their doors
when they saw us coming

threw my stuff on the lawn
piss off kid
make your own life now

never missed that shithole house
Mum had us
picking mould off bread

not made of money kids
perfectly good

didn't ever see her
lift the bag to her nose
take a whiff of the rot.

'I'm going out'
I say to Indie

'Do some school work
might bring back something nice'

Indie smiles
thinks I'm some fucking hero
doesn't know what I've done

just to get to this place
or what I'm gonna do
to keep us here.

Go back to the tracks
stupid thing to do
11 o'clock on a Saturday

people heading in to town
looking for something lively

bunch of kids
hanging round the platform

don't see me glancing over
at the tracks
the scrub

don't know what I hope not to find
traces of myself
from the night before

wouldn't look here
won't come looking for me.

Best thing about the Gabba
ten minutes walk
a pub on every corner

walk to the closest
find a dark place

find myself again
in a double shot scotch

group of people comes in
all laughs and pats on the back

don't look around
at what I'm not missing

but I hear her
and I know it's her
I know that laugh

then I look
I know those legs
that arse

I know her out of uniform.

She's with her cop mates
light beers all round

most of them look too young
too pretty
to be messing around
in the jaded lives of crims

why aren't they all
making a living
picking daisies?

don't try hard
to stop myself
from looking over

those arms
more toned than I remember

she's taller than the rest
and darker

she catches me not looking
excuses herself
slides in next to me.

'Bit early for that' she says
looking at my double shot scotch

'Bit early for policing' I snap

'You keeping out of trouble, Ana?'

'Was never in trouble to begin with,
Sawyer'

'Good' she says
looks at me a while
makes me remember those grey eyes

not as hard as she'd like to think
I know her soft
I know her broken

'Haven't seen you in a while
things been all right?' she says

'You asking as a cop
or a friend?'

'Both'

I scull my drink
'Just fine, Sawyer
aren't you a bit old to be hanging around those
kids?'

'Good seeing you' she says
standing up

I'm too choked up in my double woes
to say

don't you remember?

Sixteen and on the verge of dropping
out of school
out of life

didn't have anyone back then
looking out for me

except her.

She was a year above me
and that's how I liked her

everyone talked
it wasn't common then
locked in the toilets
with your best mate

not talking about boys
or fixing your makeup
just fixing each other
hands pinned against locked doors
people heard things
people knew

Sawyer didn't care
I'd got her good

she knew I was trouble
even back then
didn't stop her chasing me
before class
after school

I didn't think much at the time
guess I had too much else
going on

didn't see Sawyer, trying
to hold me so tight

I couldn't fit
where I used to
didn't see her eyes
her sympathy

didn't see her hurt after I
dropped out of school
off the chart.

Sawyer and Ana never existed
at least
not until I left

then it hit me

ever since
we've caught up again
tried to brush over it

just some fun in the girls' toilets
something rough to
fill our time

didn't ever try to hold on
to any of that

couldn't

if I did
might have kept me straight.

Now she's chasing me down streets
watching
I'm out of trouble

and I know it's cause she doesn't wanna
take me in

doesn't wanna be close again
knows we have unresolved business

but I have no business
trying to finish it
not now anyway.

She keeps looking over
she laughs
holds her beer in a way that says

I've got it together
I won't take your shit

she's showing the young cops

but I know it's me
she's talking to

I see her glance in my direction
more than once

and I stick close to the corner

so I don't go over there
so I don't grab her waist
and take her home again.

The last dregs of summer
dripping
from the last pub
before home

sun setting
sky meets land

trying to remember

the things I once found
breathtaking.

Indie's locked up
in her corner
studying

doesn't see me come in
go to the bathroom
lock the door
throw up in the sink

Sawyer will be all over this
once she finds out
once the neighbours complain

about the smell
coming from
his street
his house

can't look Indie in the eye
kid knows me too well

she'll see it
dark and sharp
the gap
I've opened up.

PART TWO
PACE IT

Keep out
of Indie's way
but not
so much
she realises
something's up
kids can sense
trouble

she will see it
in the way I don't
leave the doors unlocked anymore
in the way
I can't stomach meat
or those shows
about law and order

sooner or later
Indie will see
the person
I've stopped being.

'Hey, Ana check this out'
Indie turns up the TV
sprawled out
on the couch
during the after-school happy hour

'Some guy was killed
few blocks away
a random attack'

her eyes widen
like our life
suddenly
got more interesting

'Could've been us'
she says
flicks the channel

I swallow my late night crime
and can't even manage
don't be stupid

it's never random.

The heat of the afternoon
intrudes
into the bedroom
as I dress
for the late shift

the light
casts parallel shadows
across the worn carpet

it's the tracks
all over again

grab my backpack
slip
into my tattered Cons

Indie is on the phone
I try to creep past
unnoticed
'Hey' she says
'Where you going?'

'Work, remember?'
Indie nods vaguely
as I unbolt the door

'That was my sister,
hey did you hear
about that guy

killed?'
Indie fades out

walk out to
the street
too quiet
for a Friday afternoon.

Indie tells me to give it up
the work day and night
says she will get a part-time job
pull her weight

do your study instead
get a good job
words Mum never said
guess she didn't
want
for us
what she
never had

don't know much
about Mum's past
something tells me

it still follows her

nothing's gonna change that.

Some customers say

I must love this place
I'm here all the time

but I'm just trying
to hold me and Indie up

so we don't fall
under my weight

what's all this for
if not Indie?

A man walks into the store
spends too long
deciding what drink to buy
flicks through newspapers
like it's Sunday morning
and he has
nowhere else to be

shakes his head
looks
right through me
like he knows

'Terrible about that young fella
killed round here
not even safe
in your own home
anymore'

he stops
but his sentence
lingers
like I should
fill in the gaps.

Stand in front
of the fridge
forgotten what
I'd come for

rearrange the magnets
in my head
if only time
could be
so easily
manipulated

take a beer out
twist the cap open
with my shirt
watch as the fabric
recoils

there's a knock
at the door
get Indie to answer
but quickly
decide against it

open the door

face Sawyer
in uniform

'Sawyer' I manage

'Hi, Ana
can we have a chat?'

she sees something
in my eyes
shock or guilt
because she relaxes her shoulders

'As friends' she finishes

'Okay' I say
unlocking the screen
I glance at the lounge room
briefly wish
to be someone else

gesture towards the couch
but Sawyer takes up at the dining table
she sighs

'Busy day?'

'You could say that' Sawyer replies
avoiding my eyes

'Can I get you a drink?
Water, beer?'

'Still on duty' she says
'Water is fine, thanks.

Indie home?'

I nod 'On the computer
or studying
she spends equal time
doing both'
I force a laugh

Sawyer remains straight-faced
place a glass of water
in front of her
notice
the crisp lines
of her
pressed shirt

the lingering
lemon scent.

Sit to face her
wrap my hands
around an empty mug
trying to remember
the feeling

Sawyer never used to be like this
I was the serious one
caught up in my head
or in trouble

I notice her discomfort
in our quiet

I ask the question
I've been trying to avoid
'What brings you around anyway?
It's been so long'

Sawyer takes a sip of water
uncurls her fingers
from the glass
so gracefully
that I wish
I'd brought my table manners too

'You've probably heard' she starts
'About the guy who was murdered
last week
not far from here'

'Saw it on the news
yeah
you going into everyone's house
asking questions
or am I the lucky one?'

run my fingers around the band
on my wrist
try harder
to sound
less like
I've got something to hide.

'I've been to see other people
that's my job
to ask questions'

'So you're not here
for a friendly visit after all?'

'Look' Sawyer stands up
'I had to ask
or at least enquire
I don't want to think badly of you, Ana'

'Then don't' I reply
standing too

Sawyer looks at me
straight

'What do you want me to say?'

'I don't know
anything
you haven't changed
you're still running
after all these years'

I stay quiet

'I'll be in touch' Sawyer says
looking at me

to make sure
I know she's serious

I watch her
get in her car
body slumped forward
with

a weight
that is not
her own.

I close the door
as she
drives away

rest my head
against hardwood

'Was that Sawyer?' Indie says
coming up behind me

I pause
turn to face her
'Yeah'

'What's up? What did she want,
you two haven't talked in ages
have you?'

'I saw her last week'

Indie studies my face
'Was she asking about that guy
the one who was murdered?'

I miss a beat

'Yeah she's asking everyone' I say
trying
desperately
to keep it together.

I walk to the soccer club
where I first saw Sawyer play
she was good
really good

we'd never talked before
but I'd noticed her
around school
hard not to

stopped her one day
after her match
told her
she looked good
didn't play too bad either

think I made her blush

Sawyer was the first girl I'd been with
could've been the last

she was the most
unforgettable person.

Sit in the stands
recall the day we met
so vividly

I'm not surprised
to find
my cheeks wet
my heart longing

for an ending
that doesn't involve

leaving Sawyer
alone on the pitch again

wondering
how we went wrong.

Sawyer thought it was easy
for me
to just pick up
and disappear

don't know what was harder
leaving
or facing her again
years later

late one night
in a bad part of town
with the wrong
kind of company

hadn't seen anyone in years
since Mum kicked me out
not even Indie

drifted between shelters
friends' couches
drifted so far away
from who I could've been

when she found me that night
I tried to run
didn't wanna get taken in
but mostly
because

I couldn't handle
her seeing me like that

Sawyer had done well for herself
not long out of school
already a rookie cop
soon rising up the ranks.

She took me
to her place that night
not the station

maybe that was
her first downfall
to believe in me again

set me up
on her couch
with a cup of lemon ginger tea
and one of her old sweaters

'Sawyer' I started

she put her hand
over mine
'We can talk about this tomorrow, Ana'

I realised then
the dynamic had shifted
between us
suddenly
I was no longer on top.

Sleep escapes me
lie awake
thinking about Sawyer
like it was
yesterday

our bodies
too close
too much

when I wake
my arm is extended
to where
she should have been

get a call early
to come in to the station

just after Indie leaves
grateful
for one small mercy

I rush out the door
leave the TV on

walk the twenty minutes
to the station
hopeful
my apparent
lack

of punctuality
is the only judgement
they make.

Sawyer is
mid–conversation
when I arrive

excuses herself
approaches me
places her hand
on my lower back

a gesture that could
be comforting
but one I knew better
than to second guess

she faces me
almost
looks disappointed

look into her grey eyes
try to find my way
out of this mess

'You okay?' she asks
her voice
cracking

I nod

'Robertson, Ana?'
a man calls from a doorway
Sawyer's hand slips away

'I'm Ana' I say
too quickly
forgetting
my manners

the man
escorts me
into a room
where
another officer waits

I sit across from them
help myself
to a long glass of water
as if time
was all I needed.

'Would you like to tell us
why
you think you are here today,
Ms Robertson?'

'Well' I start
'I was hoping you could tell me that,
officer'

the two officers
exchange looks
clearly
not as trusting
as my dear Sawyer

'Ms Robertson
where were you
the night of
Friday
March 1st?'

'At home
with my sister'

it comes out
so quick
I almost
believe it too

'Will your sister
confirm this?'

'Yes'
I swallow

'Did you know
Mr Dylan Sanders?'
the officer asks

'No, sir' I reply
my ability to
lie
convincingly
on autopilot

the officer holds up
a recent photo

push my nails
deep
into my jeans
stifle
my natural
reaction

'A local man
he may have come
to your work

you may have
seen him around'

I shake my head
knowing
it isn't a question

the two officers
stand
'Okay, Ms Robertson
that's all
for today
we'll be in touch

let us know
if you
think of
anything'

I nod
try hard
to swallow
my relief.

Sawyer drives me home
punishes me
by saying nothing

I glance over
at the cool way
she goes about life

she frowns
as if
I've already been
charged
convicted and sentenced

'Didn't think
we'd be doing this again
so soon
did you?' I say

as if this is stand-up
and I'm the punchline
Sawyer has missed.

Sawyer pulls in
to the drive

'Thanks
for being a friend'

Sawyer grimaces
I open the door to leave

'I hope I'm right
about you, Ana'

I turn and look at her
'Me too.'

Grab a suitcase
from under the bed
covered in dust
reeks
of my childhood

throw in anything
that's close
almost smile
thinking
life doesn't ever
seem to change

not too long
since I last did this
what was that
Sawyer said
you're always running, Ana

does that mean
she wants me
to stop?

does that mean
she thinks about it too
what we could've been?

don't pack much
what is there to keep

of a life
lived like this

leave room for Indie
but don't think
I know
the small things
she has treasured.

Indie gets home
quick to notice
the dust has stirred

'You taking a holiday?'
she says
gesturing towards
the half-packed suitcase

'Get your stuff
we've gotta leave' I say
running circles
around the house
around myself

rummaging through
stacks of papers
mostly Indie's junk
and the inevitable
debris
of suburban life

'What are you looking for?' Indie asks
following me

'Nothing
why do we have
so much
fuel for a fire?'

I find it
on the bedside table
where I left it

the only
meaningful gift
from Mum

a tattered
second-hand copy
of *The Outsiders*

maybe
it was Mum's way
of telling me
I fit
somewhere.

I pile in
more stuff
necessary
for a quick exit

Indie grabs me
demands a reason
for this
onset
of madness

'Ana' she says
holding both my arms

'Are you in trouble
is that it?
I can't leave
what about my exams?'

'Shit' I sigh
sinking
into the couch
head in hands

Indie sits
wraps an arm
around me

is this what I call
looking out
for my kid sister?

I turn the TV on
loud
Indie looks worried

'I had no choice
he wanted money
said he would hurt you
if I didn't get it
I just went
to talk
but he—'

the phone rings
Indie startles
'Leave it' I say

'Who, Ana?'

'Dylan, a guy
I used to know
he hooked me up
with stuff'

don't stop
to consider
the kid
too young
to hear this

remember
growing up
in this family
you grow up
fast

'He had a gun
I didn't
mean to—'

Indie gets up
walks to the kitchen
starts piling plates
running hot water

'Things were good, Ana
why would you
mess that up'

'I know
I'm sorry'

'Is that what you'll say
when they come
asking questions?'

Indie pushes a plate
into the water
watches it sink
begins to sob

'I don't wanna go back
they'll make me go back'

I hug Indie
try to be
the protector
I never had

'I won't let that happen
we just need to
think.'

I don't unpack
still convinced
I'm going away
for a long time

as dark creeps in
shadows my hope

Indie and I
devise a plan

we might have read
in
covering your tracks 101
for dummies.

We time it right
leave
the house
after the
shudder
of the 11 o'clock train

make sure
we are
unremarkable
in the night

Indie trails behind
trying not to
look like
an accessory

not our usual
family night out.

Climb

rusted wire fence

keep my head down
to avoid
ending up
on a security monitor
miles away
where the guy keeping watch
has seen

too much
he can't take back

I help Indie
but I know
it's me
who needs it

Indie leans close
and it's this
closeness
that led me
to this place

'Where is it?' she asks

I point blindly
into the scrub

push through
knee-high grass

never thought
I'd see the day
my kid sister
follow
in my footsteps

fall to my knees
knowing only
that this is the spot
where I left it

it's here
the tracks merge
form one
long
straight line
into darkness.

Breath is heavy
in my chest
my ears
attuned
to keeping quiet

fumble in the scrub
like you might
look
for lost car keys
but
with the urgency
of a lover
running late.

Hands
rough and raw
from scratching
the surface
too long

always
coming up short

'It's not here, Indie
it's not here'
desperation
chokes my voice

I'm there
again

against the wall
his hands
on my throat

and the realisation

the gun
is gone

they came looking here
next
they'll come looking
for me.

We get home
I don't bother
with the lights
defeated

just wanna
shut out
the night

but Indie comes in the bedroom
wants to
talk about it

'Maybe we were
looking
in the wrong place
we'll go back
tomorrow'

'It's gone, Indie'

don't mean
to be short
but her
false optimism
cuts me open

Indie wants
to believe

what she knows
isn't true

we're both
running scared
from a life
we didn't
bargain for.

Weeknights at work
crawl

no customers
over half an hour

silence helps
numb the mind
but not
slow
the quickening
pulse

pick up
the local paper
flick through

littered with
the usual stories
of local heroes
dog saves the day

advice on how to
dress appropriately
aimed at women
written by anonymous

almost
skip over it

my name
second-hand news

'Local police search
inconclusive'

do those words
jolt
or stutter
my heart?

Inconclusive
could mean

the cops
didn't find the gun

or
they did

but no trace
was left
of a decision
I'll never forget

a customer walks in
buys a few
nondescript items
enough to
get through the night

I drop his change
all over the counter

the man
sighs
like I'm a
good-for-nothing
checkout chick

watch him leave
then
toss the paper

know tonight
will drag
like a freight train
crossing country.

Open the curtains
to two uniforms
approaching

scan the room
quickly
might be the last time

open the door
Sawyer stands
behind her partner
distracted
by long dead
pot plants

lets her partner
take charge
careful
not to appear
one way or the other

he reels off words
like
murdered
connections
to the station now
for questioning

pulls the door shut
escorts me
to the back seat

this will
give the neighbours
something to talk about
over dinner
with their
neat families.

Not a long drive
but when you're

as guilty as I feel
and exchanging
unsure looks
with Sawyer
in the rear-view

well
I've lived this day
twice over

something
in Sawyer's silence
worries
as if
she already
knows too much

spent the night
turning it over

the question

and what to do
with the answer.

Sit me down
in that cramped room
again

cramped only
when Sawyer
enters
takes a seat
avoids my eyes

and I want
nothing more
than to have her
alone
in this room
in any room

her partner
grills me
can't help
but wonder
why
Sawyer is suddenly
gutless

always thought
it was the uniform
the badge
that made Sawyer
strong

now I'm not so sure
is it just me
that makes her
weak
at the knees?

'Ms Robertson'
Sawyer's partner starts
trying

too hard
to appear
the man in charge

but
it's Sawyer
who commands
my attention

'We have reason
to believe
you had connections
with the victim
murdered
last fortnight

you two
knew each other?'

I shrug
'I know a lot
of people
not a crime
is it?'

her partner
frowns

'We have you
on record
telling us
you did not know
Mr Sanders'

he stands
paces the room
calculating

I glance at Sawyer
begging her
to
meet my gaze

her partner sits
on the edge
of the table
next to me
looks down

'I could charge you
for lying to police
impeding
a murder investigation'

he looks at Sawyer
emotionless

take it all in
with a knee-jerk
reaction
almost
reach
for her hand

'I hope you
don't
have any holidays planned'
he says
with a smirk

I've become good
at ignoring
my instincts

so I rein it in
rather than
giving this guy
a piece of my mind

besides

only the guilty
protest

Sawyer's partner
serves up a ride home
with his
smug
dose of justice

tell him
I'd rather walk

watch Sawyer disappear
into her office
without so much
as a disappointed
parting glance.

They tell me

not to leave town

but give me
enough freedom
to lie awake
at night
wondering
when

they'll come knocking.

A loud banging
I wake
in a sweat

'The door, Indie'
I mumble
into the still room

don't ever
get this many
visitors

already
tired
of the endless
meet and greets
bringing bad news

I fumble
for a t-shirt

briefly
let myself
hope
it's Sawyer
out of uniform.

'Open the bloody
door, Ana
I know you're in there'

the voice
distinct
not one
I'd easily forget
even after
all these years

I hesitate
what gives Mum
the right
at this hour?

open the door
nearly
knock myself out
with the force
years of
pent up anger.

Mum pushes past
'Where is she
where's my daughter?'

'The one you kicked out?
I'm right here' I say

she doesn't bite

'Indie, where's
Indie? She's
coming home
with me
her mother'

'Keep it down
or get out'
I say

she comes close
gets in my face
takes a long drag
on her cigarette

watch the
rings of smoke
escape her lips
hang
suspended

I push her back
not hard
but enough
to show
I mean it

'Indie lives here now
her life is good
I look out for her'

Mum laughs

'Hear the coppas
are after you'

'Like mother
like daughter'
I say
feel the uprising
in my chest.

Indie must be
hearing this
kid can't
sleep
through a tornado

'You've put us
through
enough
don't you think?'

'Mum?'
Indie appears
in the hall

feel it
in my chest

the slow tear
of muscle
built up for years

that could
in a second
be ripped apart

Indie
looks
and speaks
like

she's been out of it
for days

Mum walks closer
I stand
guarded

'Come home, Indie
Scotty's gone
you can have your
room back'

have to give it to Mum
makes
quite a case
for an unlikely
shot
at redemption.

Don't want to
tell the kid
how it really is

make her favourite
mac and cheese
sit her down
at the table

push the food
around my plate
Mum used to
hate that

'I'll finish it'
Indie smiles
'If you can't'

I give her
a weak smile
in return

'I don't wanna
live with Mum' she says
helping herself
to my food

feels like
I'm watching myself
in a movie

forgetting
my lines

'I won't make you'
I finally say

'Will someone else?' she asks

I shrug
don't encourage
the thought
that she might
have no choice

when Sawyer and her partner
knock in the night
take my arms
behind my back
and haul me off
into the unknown

'You don't have to
go anywhere
you don't want' I say

look up
from my plate
kid knows me too well

sees right through
the act
but smiles
with some hope
that I do have
all the answers
after all.

That time
of the season
the sky
brilliant blue
before nightfall

the cold
chases
the day
at both ends

Indie's out
at a friend's

I don't do well
alone
at night
not anymore

something mocking
in the silence
a feeling
that pulls me
tight
from all sides
lets go

leaves me slack
awake
exhausted

have to stop
Indie
leaving.

A night off
no work
no Indie
but still

the guilt
nagging

turn on the TV
for white noise

check the doors
the windows
even those
that never opened

there's that car again
across the street
been there
all week

keep telling myself
guilt
breeds paranoia

but I look
again
know it's her
from the way

she sits
upright
ready to go
at any moment
the way
she
tucks her hair
behind her ears

like she did to me
once.

Don't stop myself
going out there
confronting her

Sawyer rolls down
the window

her face
lit
under streetlight
something familiar
in those eyes

I'm ready to launch
into my
I know my rights
to privacy
speech

when she says
'Get in the car, Ana'

always
had a soft spot
for the way
she whispered
my name at night.

Sawyer leans over
unlocks the passenger side
she's not
in uniform tonight

the air in the car
warm

sink into the seat
glance over at Sawyer
take in
her scent
and the way
she bites
her lip
when thinking
too much

but this isn't
the movies
and Sawyer doesn't respond
to my lust

instead
she turns up the radio
says
'I know it was you, Ana'

the words
fall at my feet

along
with any hope
this would just
disappear.

I play coy
which lasts
a whole thirty seconds

'I found the gun
it has your prints
I know
you knew that guy
you—'

I say nothing
not prepared
to go down for this
in Sawyer's car

'They never found
a weapon' I say

Sawyer looks down
and I see it
she still cares

'I have it' she says
sighs
grips the steering wheel

'Why didn't you
take it to your boss
dob me in
it's what I deserve'

Sawyer drops her arms
'Because
I care about you'
looks me in the eye
for the first time
in weeks

'I wanted
to see you
to talk
to know
why'

I'm on the
defensive

'So you stalk
my house at night
to find out what?'

I reach for the door
Sawyer grabs my arm
'Don't go.'

Lost count
the number of times
Sawyer took me in

maybe that's why
she became a cop
to make a living
from having
a hero complex

I took off
for good
when Mum
kicked me out

didn't leave
so much
as a note
for Sawyer

didn't say where
I was going
think I knew
I wasn't going anywhere

didn't wanna
drag
her down too

she was smart
had her shit together
still does

don't know
what she ever saw
in someone like me.

Shake off
the thought
this is all
an elaborate setup

the cops
using my feelings
to trap me
into making an admission
of guilt

'I want to help you'
Sawyer says
and I want
to believe her

it's easier to trust
when she's
out of uniform

and her hand
still lingers
on my wrist

for the first time
since it happened

I'm not thinking
about the cops
finding out

taking me away
or Mum
taking Indie

Sawyer floods my thoughts
leans in
kisses my mouth
hard
intensity
I hadn't expected

when I catch
my breath
but not
my thoughts

I say
'Come inside.'

Chest is
heavy
like a mouth full
of winter air

is this how it feels
to have a
conscience?

let Sawyer
take the lead
that way
if it comes back on me
I can say
she pushed me
first.

She has me
up against the wall
and I've been here
more times
then I wish to recall
lately

but not like this
not
for so many
forgettable
years

the gap
between her jeans
and her hip bone
gets me
every time

her lips
hot
on my neck
so much
I want to say

but Sawyer
pulls me in
hard

catches
my apologies
my excuses
releases them

holds me
tight
trying
to make up
for lost time

I lose
myself
in her

I'd forgotten
the feeling
of
weightlessness.

Wake up alone
tempt
the thought
of her
walking in
wearing nothing
but my shirt

but the covers
are pulled up neat
on her side

the clothes
gone
from the floor

her boots
not at the door

I get up
look for a note
something
that tells me

she was here
last night
with me.

I still feel her
for days

the way
walking the same streets
for years
becomes
automatic

Sawyer's body
her movements
felt
easy

not burdened
with what we
should have
said
should have
done

a softness
in her
that only I
was witness to.

Find my way
out of the haze
of that night

come up against
the uncertainty
slowly creeping back

not even
a whisper
from Sawyer
for days

she has motive
she has a weapon
she has
the evidence

is she
trying
to break me
like I broke her

maybe she's skipped town
doesn't want
the shadow
of her actions
to follow her
like it follows me.

I lie low
go about
dull life
like
I've never
stepped on the
wrong side
of the tracks

still

the same
questions

keep me awake
late in the night

after Indie has crashed
after I've
checked the windows
too many times
not to care
if Sawyer's car
is there.

See Sawyer
pull up
out front

stop myself
from rolling out
the welcome mat

sit on the couch
take my time
answering the door

I've never been
the clingy type
until now

hide my smile
behind small talk
don't notice
the papers in her hand

until Sawyer
says 'Ana, stop
maybe you should
sit'

'What is this?' I ask
regret inviting
bad news

she sighs
deep
like the night
we were
together

but this sigh
tinged
with disappointment
sympathy

pull at the hem
of my shirt
a loose thread
and the realisation
I've let everything
unravel.

Sawyer smooths her hands
over the creases
in the paper
where
she's clutched it
too tight

'Your mum
came in
the other day
said you were
keeping Indie from her—'

'That's bullshit'
I interrupt
and feel myself
come undone

'Legally
she has rights'

Sawyer hands me the paper
'I'm sorry'
she says
places a hand
on my knee

I reach for her
but she pulls away

stands up
adjusts her belt
tries
to re-establish
her diminishing
authority
over me.

'I just came
to let you know
you and Indie
have a week
arrange it
with your mum
otherwise' she stops

'Otherwise?' I push

'We will have to step in'

'So that's it then
I have no rights?'

'I'm afraid not, Ana
when Indie is sixteen
she can decide'

Sawyer moves towards the door
my heart pulls

'What about us?'

she turns
looks at me
and I know

'We can't
my job—'

'Can't be seen
hanging around
my type
I get it'

I pause
allow space
for her
to change her mind

'You have a week' she says
shuts the door
on me.

Not like me
to get
caught up
in emotions
like this

not since
that night
have I felt
the weight of my actions
press down
so heavy

I let night fall
quiet

don't think twice
to ask
when Indie
gets in too late
on a school night

when Sawyer
ignores my calls

when I miss my shift

I sink
into the sheets

stare at the ceiling
push apart the walls

lose myself
in the gap.

PART THREE
SMOULDER

Indie packs
the suitcase
that was my only
escape plan

try to ignore
the tears forming

I sit on the edge
of the bed
feel a strange urge
to offer her
hope

then I remember
Mum
and her
revolving door
of unsuitable candidates
for stepfather
of the year.

I'm convinced
Sunday afternoons
were made
for leaving

Mum rocks up
in a beaten-up
Corolla

doesn't bother
getting out
never was
one to do
what was expected
of her

hug Indie
tight
'I'm not
leaving the country' she jokes

'I'm sorry, Indie' I say

waves me away
like I didn't
have a
choice

like I'm not
the reason

she has to go back
when we both know
better.

Is that what life
was like
for Mum too?

when another boyfriend
trashed the place
took off

left Mum
on the floor
in tears
saying she wants
a gun
to take away the pain

me and Indie
curled up on the bed

I'm covering her ears
telling her
it will be okay
whole time
not noticing
the tears
down my own cheeks
the fear
of being left alone

is that what Indie
implies

when she
waves me away

that I didn't
have a choice?

like Mum never did
all those years.

Collapse
on the front steps
don't worry
who will see
me broken

in the distance
the Gabba lights on

people flocking
to the footy
or
the cricket

all the same to me

tell myself
Indie will be okay
they are probably
home now

Mum might have
set the table
dusted off
the salt and pepper
shakers

dug out
the tablecloth

at the very least
made
a vague impression
of home life.

Return
to my old haunt
but find
no comfort
drinking alone

see her
when I walk in
alone
staring down
the barrel
of her drink

my body
not yet
accustomed
to staying
away

look too long
she catches my eye
waves me over
orders two more
of what
she's having

I sit to face her
the space
between us

almost
too much.

The warmth
of the pub
wraps around my
whole body

not many people
come here
guess that's why
I like it

'On a break?' I ask

Sawyer shakes her head
'They took me off
the case'

she lets the words
fall out
too easily

lay my hands
out
on the wooden table

'Why?'

'Why do you think?'
she challenges

'Someone found out
about us.'

I stop
Sawyer
lining up
another round

'Time to go' I say
put my arm
around her shoulder
lead her out
of the pub

warm
from the alcohol
downed
with such conviction

the hope
that loss
might be easier
to grasp
if you can't recall
what it is
you are losing

just the feeling
I can't escape
feeling
responsible

for Sawyer's
downfall.

Back in school
Sawyer never said much
about her family life

probably got sick
of mine
intruding
on our time

know her mum died
young
an only child
her dad was
protective

maybe that's
where she got it from.

We stumble
into the night
with such
reckless
abandon

almost
let myself believe
this is
our life

Sawyer clings
to me
to keep
grounded

have to
stop
any impending
sense
of hope
that this
is how our story
ends

'I never stopped
you know—'
I hesitate
choke

on unresolved
feelings

'I know' Sawyer replies
'Me neither'

squeezes my hand

I instinctively
pull away
from affection
that is
misplaced.

The sky
shot with stars
don't get many
nights like this

Sawyer leads
down her street
where
the lawns
and the ladies
have matching
manicures

where
on collection night
the paths are
neatly lined
with bins

not tipped over
revealing
questionable
contents

Sawyer opens up
I pull back
burdened
with a newfound
sense
of morals

'Aren't you coming?'

I look back
into the night
too used to having
something
to hide

'Is that a good idea?' I ask

she shrugs
disappears
into the dark house
pulls me in
pushes
her lips
against mine

laughs a little
like we're
sixteen again

and the only thing
to shorten
our breath
is the thought

of getting caught
before class.

I stop Sawyer
taking it further

'You should
sleep this off' I say

pull back
the covers
on her bed

not with
the same
urgency
as I had
pulled back
my own
to let her in

I turn
to leave
as Sawyer looks set
to forget
this night

'Will you stay?'
she asks
before
closing her eyes.

Sit on the side
of the bed
contemplate
her warmth

take
what might be
my only chance
to look around her room

find comfort
in the lack of
photos
and personal effects
so like Sawyer
to live
simply
honestly

bend down
take my shoes off
knock my foot
against something
under the bed

lean down
pull out
a shoebox

inside
the gun
my gun
his gun

look back
at Sawyer
unresponsive

almost see
a way out
something
opening up

I could take it
right now

press it
close to my skin
under my shirt

leave this house
get rid of
the damn thing
that's caused all this.

There's danger
in the quiet
of night

lie next to Sawyer
tense

don't invite sleep
that would mean
I've missed my only
chance

Sawyer rolls over
instinctively
flings her arm
over my body

I want
nothing more
than to
encourage the gesture

regret
that she
has seen me
at my worst

so few times
since we met

have I been
at my best.

Watch her chest
rise
and fall

mimic her
breathing
with my own

consider
one last time
making
a quick
escape

I know
with first light
Sawyer will wake
wonder
what is it
I'm doing here

if I wasn't
who I am

if I hadn't
done

the things
I've done

she would
ask me
to stay

we'd eat
a conventional breakfast
talk about
our mundane
lives

can't quite believe
I'll ever
be that person
for her

so why then
can't I
get off
her bed
take the gun
leave

erase

all traces
of my impact
on her life?

When Sawyer stirs
I tie my shoes
turn to look
at her

it's not surprise
in her eyes

but something
I can't quite
describe

'You leaving?'
I nod

always did
leave
before
I was asked

she leans
across the bed
takes my hand
'Thanks for getting
me home
safe'

'You would've
done the same
for me' I say

my back
half-turned
I feel her gaze
fix

the sudden urge
to leave
before
she asks
something of me
I can't give

'Things could've been
different'
she lets go of my hand
'If you stayed'

'I know' I say
'But I didn't'

I get up
with no care
for what that means
or where
we could go
from here.

Work at the café
busier
than usual
thankful for the
distraction

so few hours
I'm unable
to indulge
in self-pity

notice
murmurs
around me

the tea
and scone ladies

short with me
look away
quicker
than usual

imagine
picking up
the local
seeing my name
in bold letters

the cops
waiting
at my door
when I walk up the drive.

Before Indie
pulled me out

got tangled up
with a girl
she gave me
a place to stay
and sometimes
company

Dylan was her
housemate's boyfriend
said he could
hook me up
with anything I needed

even get me
some jobs
dealing
on the side
for cash

this girl reassured me
it was nothing
serious
no one was getting hurt

that was her
fall back
sense of morals

that let her
sleep easy

guess it was easy
back then
to live
every day
not bothering
with the complexity
life might hold

tried not to
think too much
about what I was
leaving behind.

Indie showed up
one night
Dylan and his mates
were over
couldn't hear her
knocking
over the music

'Indie' I said
'What are you doing here?'

I'd been gone
five years

it showed
on Indie
my absence
could feel it
in my gut

my kid sister
all grown up
and I hadn't
stuck around
to see it

she looked
as ragged
as I felt

'Can I come live with you
please?
Mum's new boyfriend
is a creep'

'It's not
that easy,
Indie
Mum will
have to agree'

she looked down
defeated

I saw myself
in her
and knew
I had to get out

thought I could just
slip out of
their lives
that scene
unnoticed.

Kick around
loose gravel
waiting for
the bus home

fixated
by a magpie
on the powerlines

watch it

swoop

for its prey
with such
measured
urgency

wonder if

getting
what I want
could be
that easy
too.

See the blue and red
before I see her
body seizes up

my mind
not quick enough
to consider
running

when I get closer
I see
it's Sawyer
alone

feeling returns
enough

to make
a mistimed
joke
about her
inability
to keep
away

'You should
keep your head down
next few days'
she says

open the door
Sawyer pulls up a chair
opposite

'Your mum came in
again
I couldn't see
what was going on
she talked
to my partner Matt

when she left
Matt made a call
said
they were
close
to making
an arrest
on your case.'

Sawyer clasps her hands
tight

feel the pressure
against my throat
almost
too much

'Why tell me?' I say

'If you
hand yourself in
now
they will be
lenient
I can help you'

'If I don't?'
I ask
not prepared
for the answer

Sawyer is quiet

if she isn't
preparing
my escape route
then

she is boxing
me in
slowly

'Who else knows?'
she asks
finally

'Indie'
her name
comes out
with ease

until Sawyer
draws lines
I don't want to
connect.

Sawyer drops me at Mum's
bang on the door

taken
back to
that night
at his house

the TV
blaring inside
him laughing
shouting at the door

swings it open
pissed off
that he's missed
the million dollar
question

'Do you have
my money?'

'No' I say

'Well come back
when you do'
he moves
to close the door

I stop the door
with my palm
push inside

'Maybe we can
make a deal'

he walks to the fridge
opens a beer

the place is
a mess
no more
than I'd expect

turns back
'Listen, Ana
the deal is
you get me
the four grand
by tomorrow night'

'Where the hell
do I get that
kind of money?
I'm working
two shit jobs
to keep a roof over
my and Indie's heads'

he smiles
takes a swig of beer

'How old is she
now anyway
fifteen
sixteen?
that's legal
ain't it?
she's cute'

he gets in my face
I back closer
to the wall

'Two grand
and throw your sister in
for a bit of fun'

his breath
reeks of beer
and cigarettes

I knee him
in the groin
drops his beer
cries out

'Bitch!'

'Stay away
from her
I'll get the
money
then you leave us
alone'

he walks
to the kitchen
takes a gun out
of the drawer

pushes me hard
against the wall
his hands
on my throat
the gun
to my head

'You owe me' he says
'I looked out
for you
all those years
got you
what you needed
didn't ask much
now you
have to pay'

the sound
of the TV
rings in my ears

breath is
short
barely rising
up my chest

'You and your
mates
got me in that
mess
don't think
you're some
fucking saviour, Dylan'

I manage
the words
feel myself
slipping

head light
limbs
heavy

find the strength
push him
hard

he falls
hits his head
on the kitchen bench
grab the gun
shoot him
in the chest

pulled back
by the force

allow a
split second

to realise
what I've done

then I
pick up the gun
and run.

Indie opens the door
my first instinct
to cringe

thinking
the years
I wasted
in this place

'Ana' she says
greets me
with an unexpected
embrace

'It's only been
a week' I say
uncomfortable
with emotion
'Is Mum home?'

Indie shakes her head
starts walking
gives me a tour
as if I'm a
prospective buyer

spent enough
time
here

already
familiar
with
the fine print

the house looks
different
maybe Mum
has cleaned up
her act
after all

holes in the walls
patched up
but not
painted over.

Indie shows me
her room
with the
excitement
of a five-year-old
on her birthday

Mum has
outdone herself
why would Indie
ever come back to me

she even let her
put a few posters up
and some blinds
a room with
a view

'Mum got me
a TV' Indie smiles

'Did you tell her?'
I ask

not letting
nostalgia
soften me

Indie flips
the TV remote

between hands
'Tell her what?'

'You know' I say
fixed
on the remote
the ease
in which
I could

slip
from one
to the other

'Don't be
paranoid
she doesn't know
anything'

'Sawyer reckons
they're close
to
making
an arrest'

Indie stops
puts the remote
down

'Shit
really?'

I nod

sit on the edge
of the bed
breathless

the running
caught up
with me

'So this is
your life now'

Indie sits
beside me

'Sawyer found
the gun'

I pause

'She knows
everything'

Indie stands

'Are you crazy
why would you
tell her?'

'She already knew'
I look down
suddenly
ashamed

Indie begins
to pace
the room

it's too small
to invite
the feeling
of being
closed in

'Well
is she gonna help you
then?'

'I don't know,
Indie
maybe this is
what needs to happen
maybe this
is it'

Indie shakes her head
tears forming

'Please
don't let them
take you'

I put my arms
around her

try
to give her
a feeling
of safety

knowing
it won't last.

Hear the car
pull up
too late
to get out
unnoticed

not in the mood
to have it out
on the front lawn

Indie walks me out
don't think
she means to
treat me
like a visitor

done everything
short of
asking me
for dinner

'What's she doing
here?' Mum asks

'This how you
greet
all your visitors?' I say

'I know
all about you, Ana

your new life
killed that bloke
didn't ya?'

she looks at me
long

don't know
what she hopes
to find
in me

whatever it is
must be
long gone
by now

her face
softens
and she looks
ten years younger

ten years
long enough
to make me
forget
the idea
of ever spending
a Sunday evening

eating dinner
with the family

maybe having Indie
home
feels like
her second chance

don't know
which hurts more

that she never
tried with me

or that
she's taken Indie
to have

another shot
at this family gig.

Walk home
in the dark
something lonely
in the changing
of seasons

the unexpected
way

the night
creeps in
closer to day
then you could've
prepared for

numb from
the cold
or loss

take something
quick
out the freezer
into the microwave

wouldn't do this
to Indie
but
I've done it
to myself

slump
on the couch
turn the TV on
avoid the news

don't wanna see
my face
up in lights

what good
is it
anyway
to try

pick up a life
already
in pieces.

The days are
slow
without Indie
slower even
after Sawyer
has
missed
all my calls

drop by her place
after work
it's late
when I knock

when I
go round the back
try the door
look through
nicely dressed
windows

later still
when I think
has she
shot through too?

Each day
moulds itself
on the last
but
is only
a shadow
of what it was

let too many
pass

wake up
realise

you don't
recognise
this life
anymore.

It's early
when she calls

whispers
down the line
comes at me
like a shove
in the chest

I clutch
at my breath

'It's me' Sawyer says

'Get the 6:09
west
to the
end of the line
I'll be there
waiting'

there's a quiet
urgency
in her voice
that tells me
not to ask

'Pack a bag' she finishes
then hangs up

hold the phone
contemplate

I have an hour.

Pack what I think
I need
can't be sure
I know

what Sawyer
has planned
for me

her voice
quiet
assured

if this
was a setup
would she have
sounded more
vulnerable

would
silence
fill those gaps
where words
couldn't?

Cling to
the backstreets
to Park Rd station

since I've
lived here
the paint shop
became a
European furniture shop
became an
American vehicles showroom

things don't last long
here
might not
be around
to see
what comes next

never thought
a place
could hold
the weight
of your
bad decisions
so heavy

almost
wipe out
every other

memory
leading
to that point.

The train station is
contemplative

not yet open
to the idea
of another day
played back
the same

catch a glimpse
of myself
reflected back
through the
glass of the ticket booth

haven't liked
what I've seen
for too long

stand at the
end of the
platform

look over
to the tracks
recall that
night
so vividly

like waking
in a sweat

knowing
it will be
hours
before
you can close
your eyes
again.

There's a bite
in the air
the kind
they spend
ten minutes
talking about
on the evening news

thankful to
have thought
to pack a jumper

get on the train
edge of the seat
until I'm on
the connecting line
heading west

call Sawyer
let her know
I'm coming to her

'I'm going to
sort things out'
are her
parting words

don't know
what

or who
awaits

at the end
of the line
been around
too long
to let myself
hope

a future with Sawyer
is what
I'm
travelling towards.

Never been
out
this far west
before

If I was
more certain
I could admire

the subtle
changes
in the scenery

softening of
the light

the muted
quiet
beyond
these carriage doors

think to call
Indie

before I lose
contact
with life
as I know it

try not
to let her
hear it

the crack
in my voice

the doubt
that still
lies behind
what I feel
for Sawyer

what I hope
she feels
for me

Indie asks
questions
I can't answer

will I be gone
long
when will she
see me again

am I
going to jail?

Travelling towards
the unknown
feels
immeasurably
long

time enough
to consider
getting off the
train
at the next
station

head back
into the city
where
the balance
of my life

swings
dangerously
to one side

or
I could stay

not run
not do
what Sawyer
has come

to expect
of me

every possible
outcome
to this
mess

feels
unacceptable

how do I

go on
carrying
this weight

preach the ways
of an
honest life
to my kid sister

when all
I can offer her
is

to run
or stay

to give in
to feeling

be consumed
by what
hurts me most
at night.

I'm nearly at

the end
of the line

as far west
as this will take

my last
chance
to turn back

passed

the train
slows

try to
shake
life into
my veins

the adrenaline
necessary
to face
whatever
awaits

outside
those doors

soak in
the quiet
moments

the faint
metal scent
of life

coming
to an abrupt
halt

before I am
reminded

one last time
to mind
the gap.

ACKNOWLEDGEMENTS

The writing of this book was very fast and intuitive, the initial idea for *Gap* impressed upon me with such intensity I had no choice other than to chase it, with equal intensity, to the end of the line.

Firstly, I would like to thank everyone involved in the Queensland Literary Awards, for their hard work and dedication in keeping these important awards going. Without it, I might not be writing these words. My thanks to Madonna Duffy and Jacqueline Blanchard, everyone at UQP for their enthusiasm and belief in this book, and for making this such a wonderful and positive experience.

I would like to thank Jane O'Hara and the O'Hara sisters for their support of the Emerging Award, and continued support of emerging writers like myself.

My editor, Felicity Plunkett – it was such a pleasure to work with you. Thank you for your intuitive and insightful approach to the manuscript. Your enthusiasm and support helped enormously in guiding me through this new and illuminating experience.

My heartfelt gratitude to Nike Sulway, for your endless kindness and generosity, unwavering belief and daily poetics. You keep me anchored.

To Ellen van Neerven, my first reader. Thank you for your support and encouragement, for picking my favourite lines and questioning them and for sticking it out at the desk with me for so many years.

Kris Olsson who I first connected with at QUT, thank you for your warmth and generosity, your gentle, inspiring encouragement to stick with it – you made a difference. To my many other wonderful teachers at QUT, thank you for your passion, guidance and belief.

My thanks to Krissy Kneen and all the staff at Avid Reader for all the work you do in supporting emerging Brisbane writers – for providing a supportive platform to step up to and find our voices. The many wonderful events at Avid over the years have helped solidify my desire to find a little place for myself in that world. I think I may have found it.

To my family, Mum and Dad, all my siblings, thanks for the memories and the many stories to tell. Keep them coming.

Finally, to my little sister, Olivia, I hope we never find ourselves in this kind of trouble! Thank you for the laughter and light. For reminding me, when I wake startled in the night, what I'm doing this for.

TARCUTTA WAKE
Josephine Rowe

A mother drives north with her young children, who watch her and try to decipher her buried grief. Two photographers document a nation's guilt in picture of its people's hands. An underground club in Western Australia plays jazz to nostalgic patrons dreaming of America's Deep South. A young woman struggles to define herself among the litter of objects an ex-lover has left behind.

In short vignettes and longer stories, Josephine Rowe explores the idea of things that are left behind: souvenirs, scars, and prejudice. Rowe captures everyday life in restrained poetic prose, merging themes of collective memory and guilt, permanence and impermanence, and inherited beliefs. These beautifully wrought, bittersweet stories announce the arrival of an exciting new talent in Australian fiction.

ISBN 978 0 7022 4930 3

THE REST IS WEIGHT
Jennifer Mills

A girl searches for her lost grandmother while her parents quarrel at home. A young architect finds herself entangled by a strange commission. A man contemplates inertia after toxic fallout changes life in a remote Australian town. A woman imagines a mother's love for her autistic son.

The award-winning stories in *The Rest is Weight* reflect Jennifer Mills' years in Central Australia, as well as her travels to Mexico, Russia and China. Sometimes dreamy and hypnotic, sometimes dark, comic and wry, Mills weaves themes of longing, alienation, delusion, resilience and love. Collected or on their own, these stories are both a joy and a wonder to read.

'Shifting effortlessly from the naturalistic to the deeply surreal, these stories conjure a whole sensory universe and the exiles who inhabit it with images that lodge in your head and just won't leave. Mills' precision is breathtaking.' Cate Kennedy

ISBN 978 0 7022 4940 2